LANDSCAPES
OF THE EXILED

ALAN CATLIN

DOS MADRES

2025

DOS MADRES PRESS INC.
P.O. Box 294, Loveland, Ohio 45140
www.dosmadres.com   editor@dosmadres.com

Dos Madres is dedicated to the belief that the small press is essential to the vitality of contemporary literature as a carrier of the new voice, as well as the older, sometimes forgotten voices of the past. And in an ever more virtual world, to the creation of fine books pleasing to the eye and hand.

Dos Madres is named in honor of Vera Murphy and Libbie Hughes, the "Dos Madres" whose contributions have made this press possible.

Dos Madres Press, Inc. is an Ohio Not For Profit Corporation and a 501 (c) (3) qualified public charity. Contributions are tax deductible.

Executive Editor: Robert J. Murphy

Illustration & Book Design: Elizabeth H. Murphy
www.illusionstudios.net

Typeset in Adobe Garamond Pro & Iowan Old School
ISBN 978-1-962847-20-9
Library of Congress Control Number: 2025931361

To Valerie who shares this life's journey

To Elly who invited us to visit Block Island in 1991

*Special thanks to Robert and Elizabeth for their work
and for making Dos Madres such a special press*

*Thanks to all the editors
who published the poems in this collection*

::TABLE OF CONTENTS::

3: DARK COMES EARLY IN THE MOUNTAINS

"There was a dream, of course,
but many of the most important things I find,
are the ones learned in dreams."
                    Renata Adler, *Speedboat*"

"Won't you be my neighbor?"
                    Mr. Rogers

"The trees looked dipped in acid-

desperate gray sky, easy
to climb"
                    Nick Flynn, "*Satellite*"

AUTHOR'S FORWARD

It was like a dream. A small dead bird on the deck. Three days, three different dead birds and we never heard any of them hit. All of them were casualties of a collision with a picture window. Twelve years of staying in the same time share apartment without a single bird death. And now three days in a row. Maybe it was an omen. A sign of some sort, but of what?

Off season folks got food deliveries from the mainland all the time once the on-island restaurants closed. During the Summer peak time the airplanes flew low, constantly, over the places we were staying as the hotel was a few hundred yards from the end of the runway. Any illusions of sleeping-in vanished at first light. They fly low over where we stay in the off season also, when the wind is right, just not as often. By low, I man maybe a hundred feet up. Maybe less.

I often travel the interior of the island in my mind, travel well-beyond what we were seeing every day on our walks. Incidents and places that were familiar, became less so the further inside I go. The giant seals on the North point that seem like stones from a distance become otherworldly, threatening when they move. Become a kind of presence that was transforming the way they can be seen, both in dreams and in real life.

One of the hallmarks of the isalnd is that it is ever-changing. The weather could abruptly shift from fair to stormy. The clearest blue sky could develop clouds, could radically shift the light tones from clear to variations of gray. Sometimes the transformation happens so abruptly you can watch it change. The formerly harmless, white, then gray clouds, turn black, rain falls, lightning scars the sky. The approaching storm from the mainland moves across the ocean toward where I am. Then, the North lighthouse can seem like something that glows; an ethereal thing that harbors the ghosts of shipwrecks past. And there are lots of those. More than anywhere else along the east coast so there are ghost ships a plenty. And ghost lights from the scavengers who sent up false beacons luring the ships onto the rocks for the bounty they contained. There are many places like this in the interior, similarly haunted by ghosts, and this is how they become surreal, imbued with strange auras that make the commonplace something else entirely so that no matter where you go, you are always someplace else.

The exiles are the mainlanders. Mostly. The kind of people you meet spelunking at earth's end during an apocalypse of the social order. I first began to meet them reading Ritsos and Transtromer, in translation, and these people, places, objects seemed a heightened kind of everyday existence that, at once is a neighborhood you lived in, and simultaneously, a place that Bucky Fuller would have erected on the dark side of the moon if he had a chance to build there.

In this place, turning over the garden becomes an act of violence symptomatic of something larger, a relationships gone toxic. The people next door ritually beat their dog, family reunions become murderous once the drugs and the school take control, couple's break up and a woman throws the man's possessions out the window, these things happened. This is where we live(d) and The Eumenides sat across the street watching everything that we did though at least they didn't use their family field glasses to do so, as the tribe of fat people up the block did. Gradually, elements become more exaggerated but equally as weird and as familiar. Here, the everyday people are strangers, are the ones we recognize as outliers, interior exiles. The weirdness of them suggest refugees from blocks of humanity that God forgot, who continued to mutate and procreate until they were a kind of race of their own.

And others are different kind of exiles, exiles from themselves like the poets in their youth who have names like Lowell and Berryman and Schwartz. What if you lived in *Love in a Time of Cholera* or a *Journal of a Plague Year*? These people would congregate at readings they gave. And what if Erica Jong's *Fear of Flying* were written by P.K. Dick? Or you worked in a place that had elements of an Antipodes Bar and Grill, not only in a dream but in your waking life. Welcome to my world.

And my nightmare. Dark Comes Early is an actual dream sequence. After the dream the only remaining pieces of it were complete darkness and the phrase, "Gladys gave me the corkscrew. You never know when you might need one." I don't drink and haven't for decades, and I don't work anywhere where they are needed. But dreams don't care. They escort you on a journey only you can take.

As I think about this particular journey, I note that traveling to nowhere is a recurrent theme in my work. One of my earliest long poems was a piece called *Marching North* which details a squad of soldiers marching into a jungle like Vietnam, encountering relics of battles fought, suffering from the environment, harboring doubt, and fear on this undefined, maybe undefinable mission, without orders or purpose beyond the marching itself. Some would say that would be like the army but that is supposition having never served. As the soldiers continue marching, they leave the jungle and gradually encounter a different kind of hostile environment; one that could only be described as True North. And still, they march on.

In the dream Gladys has a kind of spirit lamp for guiding the narrator up an incline that seems like it could be a mountain. And yet there is no real light, just hard to define objects, and voices, in the all-encompassing night. It is as if someone had drawn a blackout curtain over the place where Gladys and I are walking and all you can hear are voices from a Beckett play somewhere in the darkness beyond wherever they happen to be. And then Gladys is gone. Maybe she was never there at all. And then there is a summit, and a kind of dawn and perhaps a town down in a valley where their might be and a place where birds are killing themselves by smashing into picture windows. The trip feels like a circle that has no beginning and no end and we embark once more.

LANDSCAPES
OF THE EXILED

:1:

LANDSCAPES

The moon is down

phantom tree limbs scratch
against the windows
and the overhanging roof
in my mind

The appliances cycle on
and off, so loud and insistent
they threaten to murder sleep

Outside, the birds have
been assaulting the picture
windows

Their collisions are like tiny
fists pelting the glass

We gather their bodies
in canvas bags

Take them to the beach
and throw them to the wind
commanding them to fly

Landscapes

Some of us preferred
the nights when trees
were on fire to the ones
where only flowers were burning

The smoke was a challenge
for breathing but after a while
we learned to live with it

Those of us who preferred
our landscapes with living things
over desolation rainbows were
disappointed when there was
nothing left to burn

Even the sunsets regretted
the absence of particulates
that made the sky seem alive

It seemed unnatural
to grieve the end of landscapes
as no one responded to them
anymore

What would have been
the point

Mornings,

as soon as it is light
single prop planes fly low
over the Neptune, landing
and taking off five minutes
apart

All summer long it is
impossible to sleep but
we are compelled to try

After months of not sleeping
we begin to hear and see
things that aren't there

In the cold months,
after the tourists are gone,
we order air delivery pizza
and they arrive still warm
from the oven

We drink beer and talk
about nothing

Overhead dozens of planes
circle the island, unable to land

Chimes at Noon

As we sat on the hill
behind the old house
not a home once a hotel

the sun was in a partial
eclipse making the light
we try to read by feel
temporary

as unreal as fragments
of objects seen in cracked
mirrors at the edges
of our sight

The grass seems scorched
in this strange half-light,
all the scrub trees are
lifeless and leafless;
death is never out of season

We read on as the Harbor Church
bells won't stop chiming
the hour

O Happy Days

Hot House

All the hot house windows
are broken now and the glass
beneath our feet is like gravel
that has reflective images
trapped inside

All the raised beds have
nothing but dry dirt,
the desiccated bodies
of weeds, unearthed
annuals, spider webbing and
paper thin wasp nests

The digging tools are
all rusted now: trowels,
spades and forks, all useless
for digging

Wild grape vines grow
through the spaces where
the glass should be,
intermingling with the stunted
berry bushes

The hum of the oversized insects
draws the heat inside

Fog

We hadn't known a fog
could be all consuming

that long familiar paths
we'd walked a thousand times
could be as treacherous as
a minefield

as an obstacle course
with immovable objects in it
or a hedge maze there
was no known solution to

Walking out, we were lost
in no time, were separated
by impenetrable mists no light
could penetrate

We called out to each other
but our voices were muffled,
were inaudible as segments
in a dream we wouldn't remember
once we woke up

Before the first floods

we used to sit
by the kill as day passed
over to night

The rushing downhill water
had a green tint to it by daylight
but at night the water
seemed to come alive

as ripples became small
furry creatures that looked
like fish with wings
that weren't fully developed yet

Disembodied voices carried
over bodies of water,
over the banks and disappeared
into the trees before we could
answer

Neither of us were sure
if the voices were speaking
to us or to someone

to something else we would
never be able to identify

The stationery rocks

at the point, where The Sound
and the ocean intersect, are not
stones but a pod of seals basking
in the sun attended by flocking
sea birds that signal our arrival

One by one, the massive creatures
slide into The Sound at low tide
to eat what fisherman used to catch
in nets

Every year there are more seals,
multiplying, inexorable as tides,
moving inland a beach head at a time

Birding

The birds are watching
from the leafless
lifeless trees

as we take the hot-
from-the-oven poison
fruit pies outside to cool

Every day the same
routine: them watching
us, inside, watching them,
as they watch, waiting
for them to land

It takes days,
sometimes weeks
before they are brave enough
to sample what
we have made them

After a few weeks,
all the birds are gone
until the next batch moves in

Don't eat the Boysenberry

Swans

On summer days we watch
the recovery swans
pair for life

The broken winged one,
healed now, has no mate

She swims in tight restrained
circles as if life has no meaning
now that she is alone

Winter nights

The trees are coated
with dry ice released
from toxic clouds

Outside, we try to breathe
through ski masks and
attempt to see though
snow goggles that render
us nearly blind to
the spreading waste of land

We navigate our way
home guided by sound,
by the snapping of tree limbs,
by thick ringed trunks
exploding from the deep cold
expanding inside

Shattered bark propels
lethal fragments that disappear
into the fresh fallen snow

An Assassination of Crows

The crows gather on
the rise above the hollow
where the stunted trees
are like scarecrows in
search of human form

An unnerving silence
of flocking birds
fills the sky with
feathers as they circle
but almost never land

Arriving at dusk
everything else living
recedes into shadows
to wait

Crow eyes burn brighter
than an acetylene flame
sparking where they touch
the sky

Redefined (Ezekiel)

An accumulation of
frozen sheep redefine
the landscape

Piles of ice, and snow
and road waste are assembled
like burial mounds planted
on the fallow furrowed fields

Dried wild berry vines
and sunflower stalks smolder
in the rusted metal burn
barrel

We look up at the sky
at what the sheep
can no longer see

Fortune Telling

Mornings we boil water
for sweet tea

Steam fogs the sliding doors
to the deck until all we can see
are the red runway lights
on the hill where the airport is

Once the tea is steeped
we remove the leaves and spread
them on plates to dry

like the entrails of sacrificial lambs
that have been offered to placate
the absent gods

Clouds

After a week of rain
the clouds fit into sky
like plaster death mask molds

the wind transforms
changing their shapes until
a panoramic sky is
a museum of dead faces
crying out in pain

If we were still looking
for answers from the heavens
we now know that none
will be found

Shadowland

The blackbirds are
messengers of death
roused from Van Gogh
wheatfields by a single
gun shot

that echoes between
mountains where Hokusai
peasants strain as they climb
into a dark sheeted rain,

a rain that scores an
Impressionist sun;
a Marsden Hartley morning
then a Charles Burchfield
afternoon in a final
Kurosawa fever dream

that needs Philip Glass
music to by finalized as film,
as end times with demons in them

Storm Warning

4 A.M. seems like
a dream to us now
that there is light
where there should be stars

Electricity splits the sky
into two vanishing points
that crack wide open snapped
like chicken bones dried by the sun

Once our eyes get used
to a new way of seeing
what isn't there

we focus on the storm clouds
where the heavens used to be

The cold sun

draws heat from the sky
and breaks down each piece
into embers of lights
that fly apart in the night

All the flood zones
have frozen and the canals
we used to travel on by boat
are impassable now

We can see where
the animals we used to eat
lay down and became
part of the ice

We wonder if we could
defrost large blocks
of them and whether there
would be anything
left to eat

Symbiotic

We share everything now
even our dreams

The details may be different
but the effect is always
the same

Her dreams are of flightless
birds that are somehow impelled
from their coops into the air
where they collide in pairs
and fall, on fire, to the earth

Mine are of the beheading
of chickens on multiple
chopping blacks propelling
their headless bodies spouting
gouts of blood as they run
about the barnyard

We watch from inside our bedrooms
where the heat pipes are bursting
in the walls releasing gushers of water
that peel the patterned paper off
in long strips that cling to our faces
as we dream

Neither of us has the will
to wake up

All of our nights are like
this now

Some of us remember

when the seasons did not
fluctuate from one extreme
to the other

There were variations
on themes: colors, warmth,
and chills instead of deep
freeze and fire

Soon there will be nothing
left to burn as it is pointless
to plant things when nothing
has a chance to grow

Maybe the end has
come and gone
and no one noticed

:2:

EXILES

The Village

The village squared, the village primed,
the village meeting beneath Dunbarton
Oaks, under the spreading whatever;
the village within the village, the unknown
village: Greenwich, Los Alamos, Manhattan
Project Village, home of los bravos, las
bravas, the village elders, village alders,
the village Dutch Elm Disease, the post
nasal drip, basal metabolism, benchmark
biologies, euphemistic eugenics: whipping
posts, stocks, and bonds for puritan punishing,
public pools for Skeffington rides, dipping
the witches, the warlocks, crucibles for
stifling deviltry in villages of the damned,
global villages, village chimes, village
churches, steeples and naves, tombstones
and crypts, village idiots, village leaders,
villagers with torches and ropes, smoking
out the aliens, revoking green cards, blue
cards, trump cards, lynching the offensive,
redefining purity, puberty, poverty, preventing
the casting of stones; littlehowtownvillages,
peaceful as hell and we like it that way, villages
a great place to visit, a better place to live, villages.

The History of Industrialization

within interlocking geodesic domes,
R. Buckminster whatever's, trans-
parent walls and non-existent doors,
rites of passages, subdivided inside
as a room for weddings, a room for
birthing and a room for death, a 2001
a Space Odyssey room, a room where
wars are planned and where they
are fought, a room where Art is made
and music is played, a room where
the conductor and the composer are
one, a room for seeing through walls,
ceilings, mirrors, where the world is
a marble globe that has no markings on it,
no boundaries, no clear definitions,
just is as music is induced from
the quivering bodies of half-jugs hung
at varying heights from ceiling hooks,
some stoppered, some not, the sound
made, uncanny, unearthly, and atonal
in such a way that a new scale must be
invented to contain it, a new globe fashioned,
one where all the rivers flow backward
and heaven and earth reverse,
as impossible as that.

New Mexican Atomic Museum as Atrocity Exhibit

The history of waging peace
in terms of nuclear weaponry
is an episode of Mystery Science
Theater, a front row table at
The Atomic Cafe for mid-fifties
training films in what to do when
the bomb drops copiously illustrated
on how to construct your very own
bomb shelters in the sanctified
safety of your own backyard or
commemorative annual parade day
pictures of the "Atomic Float"
glorifying New Mexico's rich
atomic bomb making history,
costumed young virgins of
the desert riding high on smoke
spewing dummy bombs, quiescent
for now, mock nuclear reactors
commentary limited to fatuous praise
of an all-mighty weapon, answering
the challenge of brinkmanship by
adding megatons, alms for destruction
to save the world from itself and
all the future generations forestalled,
to build an altar for ground zero,
targets for government sanctioned
cultists of death: to control arms
we must build them, more arms mean
more might, ignoring the consequences,
that an atomic bomb is forever,
if we really knew what we were doing,
how could we go on?

After the Fire, Desert Rock, Nevada, 1955

after reading Paul Zimmer

At Desert Rock, the Army doesn't
inform you what they are testing atomic
bombs for except to insure America's
future security, a future in which
the sight of mushroom clouds means
annihilation instead of the more simple
instant death brought to you by more
conventional weapons. Why soldiers are
needed in the immediate area of these
explosions, when all they can do is
duck and cover themselves the best they
can in slit trenches, is unclear. As is
the designation of this duty as Heroic,
subject of newsreels, magazine articles
and television specials hosted by the biggest
names possible: John Cameron Swayze
and Dave Garroway, is also unclear though
off-stage whispering suggest that the real
reason live soldiers are being left in shallow
trenches while after-bursts scourge the area
with fireballs, radioactive dust clouds and
deadly windstorms, is the need for human
guinea pigs; how much can an individual
conscript survive in the field during this
kind of attack? The Desert Rock tour of duty
lasts eight blasts: above ground dropped from
aircraft, detonated from blast towers and
from directly on the ground effectively
destroying full scale model Doomtowns as

film from strategically aligned cameras will
clearly show. No one knows the exact nature
or the repercussions of what was tested under
ground. Official documents covering the hazards
of doing Official Duty here cover the dangers
of deadly insect bites, snake poisons and reptile
wounds though virtually nothing is said about
the hazards of radiation exposure. Years later,
inquiries about the toxic levels of rad exposures
are met with a bureaucratic shuffle, the modern
equivalent of lying: All records regarding that
particular field of endeavor were destroyed in
a warehouse fire in Kansas, though the after—
effects linger in those hardy enough to have survived.

On Any Afternoon

women stand next to low brick walls,
gesturing toward retractable clothes lines
laden with wash, hands stained from peeling
fruit, coffee spotted shirts and jeans,
steam fogged windows, twelve-quart sauce pots
hard boiling on gas fed industrial stoves;
they could go on for hours, pointing out
the failed beds of hybrid roses, the yellow
rings of death on the sodded lawns,
black crab apple trees overhanging the sunken
meadows between estates, they could go on
long after the last glass has broken and
the houses filled with smoke, the smell
of scorched pots, burnt fruit, scalded flesh,
they will go on and on and on, nothing
can stop them.

Chronicle of the Exiled

A change of residence in the old neighborhood
meant violence, broken furniture, the family
photograph album thrown in the street, trod upon
by neighborhood dogs, lingering feet.
Later, turning the weathered pages, the torn spine
unbound, cigarette holes Confirmation Days,
mother's eyes smeared black and white ash,
mixed media with mud, wedding days burnt
through, successive years of childbearing,
family picnics, feuds, generations of black
holes; a nine-year-old child is waving to someone
on the last page, his face crippled by loss,
a hand held is missing, there is no forwarding
address.

After Every Death

One more night trying to blow out
the candle flame, lips pursed, reflected
in the engraved bureau mirror, blowing back,
stiffening the flame, the black ringed eyes
of not sleeping. In the bed, the prone figure
of a naked woman, tattooed buttocks, twisted
white nightgown knotted at the waist, stained
sheets lying next to the burst feather pillows,
a fishing knife blade embedded in the wall;
outside they have been hammering for days,
building scaffolds, how long can it go on
like this?

The Empty Window

She is throwing all the furniture
from a second story window, first,
an end table, followed by a lamp,
a transistor radio, still playing,
a large electric clock, cordless
telephones, the VCR.
Stuff is piling up on the sidewalk,
cascading into the street, still,
she keeps dumping: a hamper
full of unwashed clothes, soiled linens,
men's and ladies underwear,
work shirts and shifts, then,
the hamper itself, lying in a pile
of leaking plastic bottles, broken glass,
torn pages from spineless books;
looking up, the window is empty,
there must be nothing left inside.

The Family Reunion

begins outside, rows of picnic tables
pushed together, steaming red hot grilles,
quick fried foods, quarter kegs of cheap
domestic beer. The children hit hard balls
over the fence, off neighboring houses,
the women are yelling: "All this infernal
noise must stop!" But the children are into
screaming games, tying the youngest's wrists
together: "Let's see how far we can stretch
them behind his back." The men are playing
Black Jack, five dollars a hit, chugging beer,
ignoring the women, saying, "We are doing
something, we're playing cards. They're kids,
they're having fun." Every year the cops are
called to break up their men fighting with broken
beer bottles, rusting church keys, gravity
knives; after the fighting, they cut down
the forgotten children hanging from the trees.

Next Door

The women are beating
the dog with rubber
mallets, wooden spatulas,
ballpeen hammers, shrieking:
"This must never, ever
happen again!" The ground
must be smoothed over
to cover all the frantic
digging, the howling must
be silenced once and for all,
the undigested food washed
away along with all the blood
and guts; each month they buy
a new dog, they never learn.

Attrition

They are into front porch
motorcycle maintenance,
greased monkeys, Pink Floyd
concept albums, Mad Dog 20-20,
heavy leather, teenage girls,
rolling monster joints one handed,
spooking the mailman, worshipping
the devil, modifying things with
tire irons, cutting up with census workers,
shoving policemen through picture
windows; one by one, over the years,
they kill themselves off.

Good Neighbor Policies

They stay up all night, fighting and pushing
each other down stairs, you can hear their
children pleading: "Don't hit me, Mommy,
Daddy, please!" The unmuffled slapping of
hands against face, hysterical crying, the old man
smashing liquor bottles in the street.
For days afterward, everything smells of
Seagram's 7, VO, Canadian Club, Calvert's Extra
Dry—, of burned-out mattress covers left out
too long in the rain before the coming of the
cops who cuff the old man on a bad check charge,
of all things, leaving her to deal with the booze,
the pills and the kids alone with ambulance
drivers, stomach pumps, social workers, welfare
systems, unsympathetic State paid shrinks.

Hangover Requiem

Broken voices speaking of black leather
jackets and motorcycle boots, twisted
heavy metal, vehicles undone, all the ess
curves taken at too high a speed, rain
slickened and oil stained, all the un-
controllable black ice skids that always
end against unforgiving stone walls,
embankments, metal guard rails and
all the lame voices expending their final
breaths trying to forestall the inevitable:
plush lined boxes, floral arrangements,
slow movements following the exacted
wrath of God, discordant solo notes
rocking the ages, hymns for all the reckless
ones dying too young.

Subterranean Dwelling

All of them that run from rain clouds,
open cellar doors, hurry down
worn steps of rock, push storm doors
aside before the elements explode.
Sliding a metal bolting rod in place
they descend stairs, slowly stepping,
hands against earthen walls,
they grope in darkness for kerosene lamps,
touching cold jars of preserves,
slimy mounds of flesh, clinging webs,
striking blue tipped matches against shoe
leather. The sudden light reveals a rising
of a newly liberated dead so long trapped
underground; fearfully turning, they find
the stairs are gone, the match light blown out.

Quarantined

All the windows are boarded shut,
garbage fills all corners of every room,
brown bags ooze liquids onto rippling
parquet floors.
Somehow, flies get in, all the unwashed
dishes have maggots, spider webs hang
from the barren refrigerator door.
All power has been disconnected,
seeing is by candle light, subsistence
is on canned goods, pets, and their food;
when the officials pound with their
nightsticks, we pound back.
After a while it is impossible to tell
tell who is trying to get in,
and who is trying to get out.

Flushing State Street

They are opening up the fire hydrants,
flushing the streets, unleashing foul,
rusted liquids, storm sewers long contained
by black pipes, suppressed wastes.
No one is allowed to wash or drink,
all water must be boiled,
and the indoor plumbing backs up.
Random houses are condemned
for burning, city streets sealed,
no one is permitted to move.
The affected houses are marked
by burnt corks; the dead are
removed at night.

The Antipodes Bar and Grill

All along the back bar shelves
are hard boiled eggs preserved
in brine, embalmed, pressed
pink pig's feet, floating pale
green olives immersed in oil,
bleached white stem cherries,
lost generations of black fruit
flies are floating in the flavored
brandies, sour mash whiskies
and blended ryes. The twisted
spines of the drinkers bend low
over the tarnished wood, tracing
their names in ice melt through
the cigarette burns in the wood,
watching the spiders web metal
ashtrays no flame enlivens, no ash.
Silently, the hanging dead descend
on long thin silken threads from
the ceiling, touching the lips of
the drinkers as they hold their
cracked shell glasses in the
stifled air.

Marathon Running

They are running down
cobbled streets, under
vanishing elms, clutching
scraps of clothing, stripped
bare to the waist, the soles
of their shoes flapping as they
come, disdaining taut, cramping
muscles, discolored skin,
groin pulls hard as knots.
Their eyes are rolling all the way
back into their heads, into
expanding brains wild with
sunstroke, fevers, and dehydration;
long after the lead runners
have moved on, the crippled
runners come, dragging their
useless limbs, hopping, one
leg strapped to their emaciated
waists. Later, still, the others come.

Old Couple Dozing

The sound of an axe, chain saw blades,
heavy equipment removing trees,
dynamite sticks exploding, gaping stump
holes a slicing rain fills.
By dusk, the old couple's porch door
blows open, slams shut, their calico
cat mews stuck in a root cellar,
windblown sheets flap on a taut clothesline
as they slip into a deepening sleep,
sensing the unburied, crowding their
widow's walk, wailing, arms spread wide,
beckoning the eyes in the storm.

The Delta at Sunset

Storm birds are swept in
with the sea, a clinging heat,
cacophonous otherworld voices,
white tipped waves framed
against the gray, slate sky,
rumbling waves, alluvial plains,
jutting points of kinetic light,
disconnected wires, dead lines and
damp sandbagged ten-foot shorelines,
thunder burst horizons, fractured
light, even the ozone layers are
burning, penetrating needles of
radioactive rain; impossible men
caught in the vacuum between delta
and storm, stunned by the falling
of a twilight moon.

Silent Spring

The sound of uncontainable waves moving
inland suggests unshakeable rumors of death
by midsummer, volcanic sunsets, new layers
of fallout dust.
We rake broken limbs, spread quicklime
on the seeded grass, watch snow pea vines
climbing the barbed wire, our green tomatoes
turn black, bell peppers cut by earth moving
worms; mornings we hear the violent
cries of the garbage men moving
among the ruins, faces hidden by gas masks,
removing the refuse from the curbs.

Dreaming of Horses

of equine heads violently thrust
indoors by the wind and rain,
eyes wide open, crazed, red tongues
extended, spittle dropping from
the sides of their mouths,
sweat glistening in emergency lights.
Reaching out never helps,
the room is always about to burst
apart, about to reveal the staggering
rows of chipped teeth, the foul
clinging breath that fogs in the night.

Those Who Came Before Us

lit candles they carried in brass holders
down cracked stairs. Cold nights we stumble
after, sleep walking, lost in a maze of altered
rooms, misplaced tables, and chairs, unfamiliar
prints, Dore lithographs, collages by Max Ernst,
storm lanterns leaking kerosene, unrefrigerated
fish heads; we open unremembered doors,
brush aside the webs, the soggy moldy papers
hanging from the wall boards, upstairs the
guard dogs are pacing.

The Visitors

sign the log book with someone else's name,
handle precious relics, step over velvet
ropes to alter the set tea service, overturn
matched antique oriental chairs, rattle the
behind glass bone china; the guards must be
coming, everywhere alarm bells are ringing,
the stairs resound of running feet as the visitors
patiently wait in the parlor, lighting their
cigarettes and cigars, removing priceless books
one by one from the shelves.

The Old Soldier's Home Before the Storm

They are propped up on the front porch,
confined to rocking chairs, held in place
by leather straps, their useless legs
covered by woolen shawls. Silently they watch
the grounds turn a darker shade of gray,
feel the black heat clouds rising in their
slow, hardened veins, see the dried trimmed
grasses pressing closer to the ground,
the rising funnels of dust and dirt
spinning overhead, cones touching down
on the gravel walk, hurling stones,
upsetting cars, the staff hurrying
underground, closing doors, the old men
leaning back, catching a hot damp breath
of dust and rain before it hits.

Trashing the Garden

They are digging up the garden,
ripping down the tomato stakes,
throwing them into neighboring
yards. She is pulling out all
the herbal roots, perennial plants,
crying over onions and uprooted
garlic. He is stomping wild
strawberries, axing the summer
squash, bleeding the tomatoes
lying on the ground. He is
covered with pulp and seeds, hacked
to the core, bleeding from the bones;
their lives cannot go on like this.

Fear of Flying

From the storm cellar doors
flung open, we can see them,
swooping in with the clouds,
flying low, casting long
dark shadows that are
impossible to avoid.
The sky is thick with them,
layers upon layers of
transcontinental bombers;
there is no end of them
in sight, the ground rumbles
where it meets the sky,
eyes bleed, glasses crack,
ear drums rupture, their coming
suggests we are all better off,
deaf and blind, than before.

Death, Sleep, and the Traveler

The way in and out is blocked
by rain, rubble overwhelms,
sand blasted ditches fill up,
overflow, passageways anywhere
are covered by roiling, muddy
water, eddying tidal pools,
floating garbage stinks like
hell, fouling swamp gases are
released. Knee deep in refuse and
shredded, sodden leaves, a traveler
tells of wasted outlands, of universal
desolation beyond belief: "It could
happen here," he says, "The rains
might never end. " As he speaks,
the earth shifts, armies of sewer
rats approach, swimming with the tide;
it could happen here, a punctured,
rupturing sky.

The Flag Pole Sitter Looking Down

Sees central nervous systems
opening up, pages of x-rays,
lighted panoramic maps, moving
model cities gradually revealed,
sensibilities heightened by
privation, elemental raging
totally exposed, streets of
alligators, all-consuming slime,
deep breathing industrial wastes,
stiff, lean muscles weak from
sitting, from staring down storms,
the humped backs of dense,
crawling fogs, chronicles of exile;
fearful of vertiginous dreams
of sleeping, he begins the last,
terrifying dream of looking up.

Man in the Holocene

First, the tree limbs freeze
against the brittle winds
of summer, then, well pumps
seize up, overheat, blow up
and faucets begin dripping
creosote, kerosene, dry ice
crystals, there is no smoking
allowed, no cooking.
The refrigerator is siphoning
all the cold into the linoleum
beneath the buckling floor,
all the inner compartments
are leaking the thawing liquids
of the dead, crouching in the
stairwells, summoning the flies.

One by One

The dead invite us to lunch,
order cocktails, tell our stories,
exchange colored snap shots
of all that was left behind.
Sometime between the white wine
with the meal and the Anisette
with the coffee, they part the
restaurant curtain, point their
yellowed stub fingers toward
the place down river where
the black birds are waiting.

Box Men

Prefer refrigerator boxes,
those large standing units impervious
to rain. Months of inner living
improves surfaces, skinned textures
that have a voice of their own.
Box men believe all breathing outside
turns to cancers on the tongue.
The box watchers believe there is
no life under box, only the image
of omnipresent cardboard houses moving
like hideous deformed slugs through
the suburban lanes of cottages,
public parks, supermarket malls
redefining the physics of space.

Astronomers, Poets, Garbagemen

They are carrying illuminated bells,
circular mirrors that catch the sun
turning night shades inside out.
Mornings, you may stand up, amazed,
there is no frame of reference,
everything that orients has dissolved,
the rest they are bearing away.
It's far too late to protest or
to yell, everything that matters
has been taken outside and lined up
along the curbside, garbage men collect,
stars collide.

The Woman with the White Plastic Watering Can
Molded in the Shape of a Swan

Stands in her garden, impervious to elements,
the changing of seasons, her pointed
rhinestone glasses held steady by a gaudy
golden chain, her house keys rattling on
the edge of a ring tied to a hand crafted
beaded belt encircling her girth.
Implacable, she advances, determined
to impel seeded banks, her turned earth
amidst sculpted plastic figurines,
giant Hummel creatures grafted to the
terraced soil banking holding back a
ravaging of soil. Almost by accident,
greenery unfolds between her statuary,
summoning scavenging birds that
descend around her, a feathering plague.

The Penitents

Walk the southwestern deserts,
ascetics seeking a purgatory in
this life, wearing coarse, black
hooded robes, dragging rough
hewn crosses down arroyo,
over alkaline flats, scourging
their bare, thin, deeply rent
backs with hemp whips, sharp
abrasives, braided fibers of yucca
plants or corded whips, tightly
knotted wood wrapped in a
punishing fist for flaying
unnaturally darkened skins,
chanting as they come, fantastical
languages, their voices weakened
by a lack of food, water denied,
there is no end to this punishment
out of doors, no expiation, just
the hollow pits of their eyes
where the deep heat of high
noon sun lingers, long after
the life force is extinguished.

Adolescent Children Growing Old

They can be heard, upstairs, raving
in restive sleep of a sorrow beyond
dreams, thoughts contained by restless
breathing brought about by chest colds,
emphysema, childhood asthmas, iron
lung confinements; blood samples
stain the ceiling, texturing the paint
that can never be removed, their desperate
cracked lips suck in, absorbing the dawn,
an ice aged cold; outside, it sounds as
if their unclipped fingernails are scratching,
scoring the window glass.

Immense Hot Air Balloons

inflate behind billboard advertisements
for Black Velvet whiskey, Coppertone
tanning lotion, Life and Accident Insurances,
canvas impelled by intensifying forced heat,
bold painted stripes and pointed stars
embossed amid logos for event sponsors taking
shape, looming, expanding as buoyant skins
stretched several stories high, dwarfing the nearby
communities, settlements the on-lookers
are drawn from, impelled by this unearthly
allure of on-rushing air and rising as if from
within the cracked earth-balloons; a bulging,
unseen power conferred, inside, they have
a life of their own.

Sideshow Freaks

are on the road, the enormous old
woman riding shotgun, peeling bruised
bananas, wearing filthy blue raincoats,
loathsome dresses, bobbed hair contained
by tie-dyed bandanas, accompanied by
an old man wearing a Western string tie
over a maroon shirt, red polyester pants,
coffee and grime stained, cowboy hat
crushed out of shape, non-prescription
glasses he squints through along with
cheap cigar smoke, looking for lane
markers on a perfectly straight highway
leading directly through one no man's land
to another, small towns for the Thunderbird
drinkers, a mirage beneath full moon,
aberrational starlight; the big tent at desert's
end an earthly paradise, the master of
ceremonies the magus of the spirit world
beyond this one, even the sideshow freaks
seem blessed by illusion.

The Dog Killers

for Sasha

Bring the youngest children
to the plate glass window,
encourage their finger smearing
prints, gross violations of
ethics, the breaking of plastic
toys kicked down center aisles;
they want them as puppies:
"Pick one out," they say, "The cost is
immaterial, whichever one you want,
it's yours to paper train,
we've got lots of bones to chew."
Smother the new one with affection,
until living toys become boring.
Move on to other objects, after an
hour they will hang the dog by its
choke collar on the clothesline
with the others.

The Eumenides

sit on their porch all summer long,
watching the locals over their daily papers,
National Enquirers, People Magazines,
wiping their necks with balled up
handkerchiefs. He chews on the end of
a lit cigar, his V-neck t-shirt exposes
florid skin, arthritic hands massaging
steam fitter's knees. She is visibly
affected by the heat, reclining at high noon,
rolling her eyes back behind swollen lids,
a dormant cold blooded reptile feigning
sleep. Nothing escapes them; revived by
darkness, they drink rounds of rye and
water. Gathering a brood of followers,
they descend upon the neighbors,
flicking their savage, killing tongues.

Sleepless Nights

Behind closed doors,
listening to dial tones
from all the unhooked phones,
twin beds illuminated by dying
lightening bugs trapped inside
sealed Bell jars, the heat moving
like an extra skin across the face
of the digital clock;
outside, metal wind chimes are
blown by industrial fans,
empty glass milk bottles are rattled
in a metal box, morning,
the dead collect

The Children's Crusade

They are shouting that the world as
we know it is coming to an end,
are holding signs painted in the blood
of sacrificed household pets, placards
scrolled in day glo colors proclaiming
the ascendance of a new order, glowing
crucifix hang from their necks over
white robes, their eyes bleeding from slits
in the fomenting night of their coming,
impelled by the cadence of inner drums,
vision guided by a third internal eye
that leads them through clouds of exhaust,
burning incense, rubber tires melting from
the wheels of overturned vehicles everywhere
surrounding them in the streets as they walk
into the arms of the authorities, who tighten
black blind folds, moments before the summary
executions in the street.

"And God Created Great Whales"

They are mounted on shelves,
clear bottles gathering dust, four masted
schooners, men of war, whaling boats rounding
The Cape of Good Hope, caught in the
violent currents, sensing the rising
herds of Humpback Whales, eruptions
of spume, the voiceless singing herd to
herd, male choruses of grief, up above
the lookout is pointing, the deck hands
are lowering the boats into the white
capped mountains of the sea, guide ropes
held in mid-motion; still vacuums of sound,
corked glass coffins float in the wake.

Poets in Their Youth

Working all night, the poet haunts
the attic work place, walking creaking
floor boards, drinking his antifreeze:
Beefeaters Neat. He pauses in his
journey of life, fusing apocryphal
thoughts, stunned by a non-compliant
foreign language, his images in flight,
this terrible elusive muse, burning behind
all his sacred villages, presaging death,
recalling all those horn solos endless
hidden years of Mahler's Ninth;
looking down through a frost-bitten window,
sudden haloes of artificial light limn
the stark light poles implanting a
dawning suicidal age of an imagined hell
contained by ice.

Fuelquest

"Just my luck." you're thinking,
"to run out of fuel in East Jesus.
Where the hell am I going to find
gas in a God forsaken place like
this?" You dig out your red and
yellow gas tank from amid the ruin
of the trunk and start walking down
the unlighted back road to nowhere,
pass the sign that says: WELCOME
TO EAST JESUS NO PEDDLERS
ALLOWED VIOLATORS WILL BE
SHOT ON SIGHT NO EXCEPTIONS
Start thinking this running out of fuel
business could be worse than you thought
but you don't see how and then you are
in the 42nd Street subway station still
holding that gas can and now you're
sweating bullets thinking they are going
to assume you are a terrorist so naturally
you think, "It's time to hit some bricks."
But you can't. All the access routes are
blocked by these Homeland Security dudes
like airport luggage inspectors waving
their wands at you like they're going to
attack, then you notice they aren't airport
security at all but the dead aliens from
Area 51 dressed in uniforms and holding
these laser weapon things like a *Mars Attack!*
movie and you're all set to freak when this
waitress at the Roswell Eat Here Diner is

handing you a menu and you're ordering
the House Special Burger that turns out to
be this green thing on a bun slathered in
lumpy cheese which isn't doing much for your
appetite but the waitress notices and says,
"Don't fret, son, food coloring makes
that burger green and the lumps in the cheese
are real moon rocks." Which, somehow makes
it all okay and after a few bites and no apparent
seizures a thought occurs and you ask,
"Hey, honey, do you guys sell gas?"
And the waitress winks and says,
"Depends, what kind do you want?"
That's when you notice all the Helium balloons
being filled and how the room is stuffed with
Hindenburg replica blimps in all colors,
sizes and functionality reminding you that
this isn't New Mexico anymore but New Jersey
and the radio newsman describing the events
outside is saying, "Oh the humanity!"
and you say to the waitress, "Never mind,
I'd rather walk."

The Laundromat Revisited

Outside, the lettering on the picture window
says, LAUNDROMAT, inside we are through
a looking glass, listening to new music,
something that threatens to transcend sound,
a personal orchestra that the maestro dubs his,
Instrumentarium, as he transcribes ancient
graffiti from the never-been-washed-walls,
finding pencil markings that to us say,
"It's January 26. I'm freezing. Ed Fitzgerald.
Age 19. Five Foot Ten inches. Black Hair,
Brown eyes----I wish I was dead. But today
I am a man----" but to him, these scratchings are
hieroglyphs he transcribes as notes on a blank
musical score in short hand by Gregg through
musical ideas by Schoenberg. This man claims
to be Harry from the Junkyards of Petaluma
and he looks as if this may be true dressed as
he is in overalls smeared by all manner of offal
and grease that he insists came from practicing
new tonalities, random harmonies found striking
the sides of rain-water-filled commodes with
specially wrapped snare drum sticks. He insists
The Odes to Commodes are a small part of an
envisioned whole, a symphony for the ages
featuring Cloud Chamber Bowls, Kitharics and
Marimba Eroicas, instruments of his own invention.
Pausing in mid-explanation, suddenly preternaturally
alert, we sense maestro has discovered new time
signatures in the cycles of washing machines,
chaos ordered by the agitating props, an Orpheus

rising amid the soap suds, his Eurydice lost, her
uncanny aria drowned by a poet of other worlds
and antiquities chanting a personal lament,
"For death is all the fashion now, till even death
be dead."

:3:

DARK COMES EARLY
IN THE MOUNTAINS

Dark comes early

Dark comes early in the mountains.
They were climbing up there, bushwhacking
as they went. Their headlamps cutting zig zag patterns
into the night. Gladys gave me a corkscrew once.
She insisted, "You never know when you might
need one of those." Tonight, was one of those nights.

Gladys always said,

Gladys always said, "Beware of what you dream.
Ignore those visions if you must, but remember,
these things have a habit of coming back
to haunt you." I don't know what she based these
kind of assessment on but, more often than not,
she was right. Not long after this warning I had
a dream that Gladys and I were in grave danger
in some dark and threatening place. She died but
I did not. Unfortunately, I ignored the dream.

After she left,

After she left, I began seeing all kinds of people
I knew who were dead. She said this might happen.
Most of them were illusions or cases of mistaken
identity. I wondered about the others.

Once the rain began,

Once the rain began, it was impossible
to see the path forward or back. After a while,
even up and down were getting confused.
I felt as if I was in the up-escalator dream
where all the stairs had stopped moving
and all the lights in the tunnel had gone out.
The air was stifling. It felt thick and smothering
like a wool blanket that scratched the skin
and burrowed its way into your throat.
There was no point in trying to move.
There was no place to go. Awake. Or dreaming.

In the wake of the storm,

In the wake of the storm, the night was
charged by downed electrical wires.
The streets sparked and the few remaining
trees ignited shooting fingers of flame
along the branches. The air smelled wet
and feral, alive like an animal no one
had known of before.

The way is blocked

The way is blocked by weathered stones.
Not exactly like a wall. Like what?
A path where stones grew instead of grass
or weeds. Stones that had sharp, pointed edges.
Peaks sharp as knife blades, slippery with moss
and mold that glowed in the incipient moonlight.
These weathered stones. That moaned as they
grew, aching as they cut through the gumline
of the earth like teeth with nowhere else to go.

The sky is septic

The sky is septic. An open, untreated
suppurating wound left too long to fester.
The fluids formerly trapped inside are
leaking out like rain. I'm sliding on the black ice
that covers everything the rain has touched.
It's like walking on sheets of motor oil,
something that is both solid and frozen
at the same time but impossible to move on.
If I don't relocate, I will adhere to where I am.
Become a misshapen ice sculpture
in a greasy downpour. Waking up here
is unthinkable.

The texture of the sky

The texture of the sky changed the night she left.
Low clouds took on the color of cinder blocks
that had been chipped and pitted by years
of exposure to elements. The way they looked then;
it seemed as if the slightest breeze would make them fall
through the clouds one after the other until none were left.

One of the objects

One of the objects Gladys left behind was
a book of runes explaining how you could
foretell the future by reading the skeletons
of birds. She left precise instructions,
hand printed, in such small letters you needed
a magnifying glass to read them. On closer
inspection, I discovered you also needed
a mirror in addition to the magnifying glass.
Now, when I look at her book, all I see is
a field guide for birds. None of the words
make sense to me.

Sometimes, when I thought

Sometimes, when I thought I had been sleeping,
Gladys would whisper secrets in my ears.
These secrets are the sounds of night withheld,
and what their absence might suggest.
When I am fully awake, Gladys is gone
but the sound of her voice remains.

Overnight, while I was sleeping,

Overnight, while I was sleeping, all the clocks
stopped and refused to move. I saw her face
in all the glass that held time in its place,
flat against the faces of the clock. I thought,
none of us would ever move again.

One of Gladys' many talents

One of Gladys' many talents was being able
to throw her voice. Even now, after she's gone,
I can hear her in the night among the many others
she has summoned to speak to me. I listen closely
to what they have to say but they seem to all be
speaking at once, in one of her special languages
only she can decode. "Wild talents," she used to say
with a smile," are my specialty. " Like the exploding
objects in the sky, the flaming trees, the broken bones.

We were walking

We were walking for what felt like forever
but could only have been hours. Both of us
heard the nighthawks' warning but it was
way past too late to heed. The air was sullen
and the breeze reeked of infarctions there was
no cure for. In the no moonlight, distances
between places were distorted and all noise
amplified. Still, we walked on. The sound
of our breathing conflicting with the comfort
of our being together. Reminders of dissonance
past was why I had come here, was her way
of forecasting the future.

Overnight, while sleeping

Overnight, while sleeping I saw her face
in all the glass the hands of time used to hide behind.
What I saw was no longer pretty, not the woman
I had been obsessed with for more time than
I cared to consider. What I saw was a distortion,
so bent and malformed, I thought I might scream
but instead, I felt an overwhelming charge of static
electricity prickling my skin, freezing me in place,
wide eyed and immobile. I thought neither of us
would ever move again.

In the dream

In the dream there were sunflowers wilting
on long swaying canes. They seemed discolored,
rotten, and unwholesome, rancid like the skin
of a dead animal left too long in the sun.
Sun flowers in the dark seemed to me
the most useless, the saddest once living things
that had ever been created. Smelled like corpse
flowers in full bloom. I leaned over to pick one
from the stalk but my hand felt as if it belonged
to someone else, bee-stung and swollen like
something disinterred.

Climbing all night

Climbing all night is what I do now.
Somewhere up ahead is the summit
but I never seem to reach it. Thrashing
through the undergrowth tears my skin
and my clothes. I hear others ahead of me
on the mountain though what they are saying
and doing is muffled by the dark.
The sentient trees know the way but
they will not impart their wisdom to me.

With Gladys gone,

With Gladys gone, all I can hear is the morning
is a white noise machine. The sound should be
comforting the way it was when she was here,
but now it had a whole new meaning as something
transformed from something salutary to something
threatening. All I feel when I hear it is the weather
changing, the stillness of the air before a big storm comes.
Once the rain and the winds from nowhere begin,
I remember it was Gladys' turn to light the hurricane lamp.
Now that she's gone, I don't know what to do.

The dregs of night

The dregs of night are an aberration of starlight
broken into pieces; into asteroid earth fire and
shattered mirrored glass. Inside the broken frame
where the dressing mirror stood are the discarded
shadows of her life. All of them are shining like
radium watch dials, chimerical, feral eyes pining
for prey.

I was cold,

I was cold, sitting just inside the cave we often hiked to,
wrapped in the trauma blanket of my dreams.
The sound of water dripping in the darkness felt like
being trapped in a place between sleep and waking,
unable to return to either place. I felt something moving
nearby in the darkness but I didn't know what it was.
I suspect I never will know, will never know anything
for sure again.

Just before dawn,

Just before dawn, I thought I saw Gladys dressed
in a Christmas pageant angel's costume, balanced on
the limb of bare-of-leaves tree. I knew it couldn't be her
as she would never be caught dead climbing in a tree
and she would have said, "I sure as hell am no angel."
Would have said it with a half-smile that would tell me
everything about how she got there and where she
would be after the sun rose.

Looking down

Looking down from the promontory,
in the half-light of dawn, onto the storm
wasted land, surveying the wrecked landscape
of downed trees, water-filled trenches where
the houses had been, everything I see seems
unnatural, unreal, suffused by the remnants
of moonglow. A fetid fog rises from the ashes
of blackened barns, burnt livestock, metal roofs
of out-buildings bent and scarred by the flames.
Some of the folded ruins form mangers
with sodden hay and animal remains inside.
Others collapsed hovels nothing will ever move in.
This is what the day dreams now, in the ultraviolet
light of a black sun rising.

ABOUT THE AUTHOR

ALAN CATLIN has been publishing poetry, fiction, reviews and the odd collage in littles, independents, and university magazines since the 70's. He can say, with complete confidence, that he is the only poet in the world to have published in *Random Weirdness, Tray Full of Lab Mice, Yammering Twits, The Seattle Review, Wisconsin Review, Descant, The Literary Review* and *Wordsworth's Socks*. He has won several chapbook contests including the Slipstream one and been a finalist in several major university book contests. He lost count after thirty Pushcart nominations and has been nominated for Best of the Net, Rhysling and Bram Stoker awards. As a poet of many voices, he has published a full-length collection reflecting his work as professional barman that included the recent triptych of Carpe Diem books: *Bar Guide for the Seriously Deranged* (Roadside Press), *Another Saturday Night in Jukebox Hell* (Roadside Press) *and Last Call for Lazarus* (Impspired). His *American Odyssey* and *Wild Beauty* from Future Cycle Press examined the American Experience. The third in this series of art and life was published by Dos Madres as *Asylum Garden: after Van Gogh.* His life and times of Diane Arbus was a labor of love brought to fruition by Kelsay Books as *How Will the Heart Endure?* An eleven-chapbook series of "movie poems" was recently completed with three volumes of three chapbooks each, plus two others separate little books including the Slipstream Contest Winner, *Blue Velvet.* The working title of those was *Hollyweird,* and extended a year's long project of social commentary disguised as bar poems called *Alien Nation.* A covid project of numbered prose like snap shot poems was published by Dos Madres as *Memories Too,* and represents what happens when the narrative impulse dies in isolation. His fictional memoir, a retirement project that began and finished before Covid, *Chaos Management,* was published by Alien Buddha. He is currently culling his vast archives for the forgotten and the lost over decades of creation. A recent discovery assembled into book form is *The Work Anxiety Poems* which includes uncollected work experience poems, and actual anxiety dreams about that experience, all of which happened after he retired.

ACKNOWLEDGMENTS

Abraxas: "Poets in Their Youth"
Big Scream: "New Mexico Atomic Museum"
Bizarra: "Quarantined," "Silent Spring"
Bottomfish: "The Old Soldier's Home Before the Strom"
Cannedphlegm: "On Any Afternoon"
Chance: "Marathon Running"
Cholla Needles: "Those Who Came Before Us"
Clutch: "One By One"
Defunct: reprint of "Trashing the Garden" originally
    published by *Tramp*
Dirigible: "Astronomers, Poets, Garbagemen"
Eunoia Review: "Mornings, "Chimes at Noon," "Hot House,"
    "The stationery rocks," "Birding," "Winter Nights," "An
    Assassination of Crows," "The cold sun"
Fevers of the Mind: "The Empty Window"
Fine Arts Society: "The Visitors"
Hampden-Sydney Poetry Review: "The Laundromat Revisited"
Impspired: Hangover Requiem
Melting Trees: "The Eumenides"
New Kauri: "Dreaming of Horses"
No Exit: "The Antipodes Bar and Grill"
Nowhere Nohow: "The Children's Crusade"
Penny Ante Feud: "Sideshow Freaks"
Penny Dreadful Press: "Good Neighbor Policies"
Poetry Conspiracy: "Family Reunion"
Quirk: "The Village"
Seattle Review: "The Flag Pole Sitter Looking Down"
Sign of the Times: "Chronicle of the Exiled" "After Every Death"
Spindrift: "Flushing State Street"

Synchronized Chaos: "The moon is down," Landscapes,"
    "Redefined (Ezikiel)," "Symbiotic," "Some of us
    remember," "Gladys always said," "After she left," "Once
    the rain began," "Weathered Stone, "The sky is septic"
Tar River Poetry: "And God Created Great Whales"
UFO Gigolo: "Fuelquest"
Unrorean: "Sleepless Nights"
Velocities: "Delta at Sunset"
Yarrow: "Man in the Holocene"
Yellow Mama: "Immense Hot Air Balloons"
Zillah: "The Woman with the White Plastic Watering Can"
ZYX: "Adolescent Children Growing Old," "Death, Sleep
and the Traveler"

Other books by Alan Catlin
published by Dos Madres Press

Asylum Garden: after Van Gogh (2020)
Memories Too (2021)

For the full Dos Madres Press catalog:
www.dosmadres.com